THE WOMEN
of
TUESDAY AND THURSDAY

(From Girls to Grandmas)

By: Shirley Ensrud

CONTENTS

For LaDonna
My Daughter and My Friend

FOREWORD

We take a look at today's women--
sometimes seriously, sometimes with tongue
in cheek. Woman is a sturdy creature, able
to be many things to many persons.

If you find in these pages your mother,
sister, aunt, grandmother, self or friend, I
shall be rewarded.

MY OWN THANKSGIVING DAY

The great pain done,
I feel lightness
of body, spirit, mind.

They bring her to me.
Beneath the blankets
I count fingers, toes;
and marvel...ten each!

I had wished for our firstborn
a nose like his father's,
straight and fine.
Hers is a button, like mine.

DAWNING WOMANHOOD

You are yourself
young miss;
no longer must you
prove something
to be accepted.

You need not
be like a boy;
rather, be
the girl that you are,
stretch to heights
of your ability,
remain feminine.

1

'91 GRAD'S '78 BONNEVILLE

She hated the car--
big yellow tank of a vehicle,
not sporty at all--
just transportation.

It took her to school,
to work, to games;
transported siblings for duty,
peers for fun.

Noah, she called it,
claimed its dimensions an ark.
Her father replaced tires,
respected its sturdy frame.

In teen fashion
she littered the floor,
seldom washed it,
drove too fast.

Noah died on graduation day,
consumed in a burst of fire,
but did not explode
as she poked about the rear seat
to rescue gifts and tennis racquet.

At junk yard, father
marveled that she was unscathed,
mother snapped pictures,
Samantha removed a hubcap,
took it home with her.

NEARLY WED

Is she ready to marry,
this sprite
who got halfway down the drive
when she ran away,
then turned back and hid
beneath a tree?

She baked blue ribbon kringla,
was grand champion showman in 4-H,
went to state in tennis
and to prom with Jim.

As a teen she left her room messy,
left her electric blanket turned on all day;
now turns out lights in her apartment
behind her father.

Is she adult enough?
Already she calls siblings
with big-sister advice.

But will she know how to bundle a baby
since she never buttoned her coat?
Can they survive on no-bake
chocolate oatmeal cookies?

Of course.
That degree in accounting
should serve her well
when trying other recipes.

FIRST GRANDCHILD MARRIES

With bandage on my toe
where new black-strapped shoes
have worn a blister, I am ushered

to first row, Grandpa a step behind.
Black tuxedoed youth seats our daughter--
producer and director--beside us.
Candle lighters ignite tapers.

Pastor emerges,
groom stands right of center,
knows not where to look.
"Wedding Song" is sung.
Bride's schoolmates, groom's sister
enter on arms of groomsmen.
Her sister, maid-of-honor,
(yesterday a chubby child,
today poised, hair arranged in swirl atop her head)
stands tall in black, slim, floor-length gown.
Scotch tape mends her hem.
Alexandra and David
carry flowers and ring for their cousin.

"Fanfare To Joy" resounds from trumpet and piano
as Sam and her father proceed to altar.
    From the time her mother was a girl
    her first child would be named Jennifer
    but in hospital they named her Samantha.
Throats tighten as she kisses her Dad,
turns to take groom's arm.

First Corinthians, thirteen,
prayers, homily, blessings and unity candle.
Groom's vows, said rapidly, are audible
in first three rows only.

"Grow Old With Me" is final song
before the sending forth--
forth into a new dimension,
a new commitment.

HOMEMAKERS' MAZE FOR BRIDES

With just one trip around, they say
is how to make a bed;
you tuck this side and then the foot
while working to the head.

Fluff up the pillows, straighten, pat,
then smooth the coverlet.
A cinch my husband's not the one
who left a bed like that!

Upon retiring lifts his feet--
the blankets flutter under;
then twists and turns to make a nest.
How does he breathe, I wonder.

At any rate, when he gets up
I may as well just face them.
Pull off the covers to the pad
and one by one replace them.

TO A YOUNG MOTHER

Buy the groceries and supplies,
wipe big tears from little eyes,
plan great menus, cook fine meals,
help the kids find misplaced wheels.

Wash those dishes, scrub the floor,
feed your kids who slam the door,
clean their bathroom, toilet, tub;
home's a wheel and you're the hub.

Mend the rips in denim jeans,
cook a casserole with beans;
if steak's in the future yet
someday you'll be out of debt.

Do the laundry, strip the beds,
sort all whites from blues and reds.
Chauffeur kids to parties, games,
try to learn their best friends' names.

If you are career girl, too,
orchestrate these tasks anew
every time your duty calls,
every time your toddler falls.

Sometimes, does it seem too much?
Are you feeling out of touch?
You'd not trade it for another
lifestyle, could you not be Mother.

FOR HER OWN PEACE OF MIND

She tucked the comforts 'round the child
then left the door ajar;
prepared herself for rest and smiled.

She tucked the comforts 'round the child;
knew that if beasties were too wild
her solace was not far.

She tucked the comforts 'round the child
then left the door ajar.

MOVING THOUGHTS IN DECEMBER

Snow tracks in with carriers
of buffets and bedsteads.
Helpers put boxes anywhere,
heed FRAGILE warnings.
We will sort it out tomorrow.

How old is this wallpaper?
Who chose the color
inside the cupboards?
I love the hardwood floors,
detest the bathroom tile.

I already miss former neighbors,
the screened porch,
even the sound
the water softener made,
like an elephant in labor.

No longer renters,
we will buy paint and screens,
repair drippy faucets.
This house will grow and change
and so, likely, shall we.

BISQUE BLUEBIRDS

They will never fly, the birds
upon my sill, still,
unperturbed,
they hold their poses;
one, wings aflutter,
the other, tail aloft,
mocking me.

I lift them carefully
before I dust. Just
momentarily
I understand them,
their pained disdain.
Their residence is sure
because they fit my
color scheme.

CRIES FROM THE HEART

I give her a drink,
sit beside her.
She moans, sighs.

Often she makes sighing sounds;
only today have they alternated
with moaning.

Frequency intensifies.
How can she emit two tones
near simultaneously?

Noises reach
a fevered pitch and tempo
then slow.

I wait, wonder,
almost hope.

Less and less--
one sound...
the other.

I hold my breath.
Sigh...moan...
nothing...

Oh joy!
Coffee is ready.

SOUL SISTERS

Dignified, with kindness,
she instructs parlor maids.
Tall, willowy,
she guides mount about the estate.
Intelligent, shrewd,
she enters boardrooms.
Poised, confident,
she meets his steady gaze.

The real woman looks up, ignores
basket of unfolded towels,
dust on table,
scattered newspapers
and, guiltily,
turns the page.

THERE ARE MORE WAYS THAN ONE
TO WASH DISHES

As youngest daughter
I wiped to sisters' washing--
they taking turns,
those decades ago.

When washing became my task,
dishpans teetered on tabletop,
water ran down my arms.
Homemade lye soap produced few suds
and teakettle's capacity
was never enough for rinsing.

I face a stainless steel sink
with lots of hot water.
Suds billow, and I am content.

My daughters have dishwashers.

TO PLEASE THEM ALL

"Nothing foreign in the dressing, now,"
married daughter warns
day before Thanksgiving.

So of course, I make two kinds:
one naked, just sage and onions;
the other as stuffing ought to be--
with apples and a handful of raisins.

CHURCH RUMMAGE SALE

We come
bearing boxes of fickleness...
last year's garments
we won't wear
this season.

We rationalize
our mission...
donate clothing
for those less fortunate
to purchase
for a pittance.

We turn
to the Mall
with glossy pictures
in our minds
of current fashion.

A SPIRITUAL EXPERIENCE

Go weekly for the ritual.
Sit back and be renewed.
While ministered to,
body and soul relax.

Emerge a different and better person;
shampooed, set, combed and sprayed.

UNTO THYSELF

Today, I bought sink mats,
smooth plastic, white
as fresh-laundered sheets.

Old porous cream-colored ones
would not respond
to cleanser nor Clorox.

It is not fun
to clean the kitchen
but I felt satisfaction
placing new mats in my
rubbed-to-a-shine sink.

I give myself small gifts--

HOME FROM THE SOUTH

Reality returns.
Northwest wind
spits at windshield.
Were hibiscus, orange blossoms
in December
fabrications of our minds?

11

Cheeks are tan,
Mickey Mouse ears lay in back window.
We really did see water skiers.
Snow in ditches tells us
we are returning
to routine, duty,
and overshoes.

ENERGY CRISIS

I've always known
there ought to be three of me;
one keeping house
with greatest efficiency,

the second for
my job, which is bookkeeping,
and one whole self
for golf, bridge and authoring.

I know now where
my energy crisis lies...
this body can't
keep up as I visualize.

WHO AM I?

I am lazybones punching snooze alarm,
housewife making beds,
wardrobe coordinator choosing apparel,
hairdresser, weight-conscious matron.

I am weather forecaster, thief
snapping sprig of lilac from neighbor's hedge,
bride treading petal-strewn path
made ready over night by slight breeze
through blossoming fruit trees.

12

I am botanist wondering what species
of wild flower is four-petaled
purple blossom with ruffled leaves,
cook coveting rhubarb going to waste.

I am artist framing in my mind
cumulus clouds in azure sky
above brick church with steeples,
blue spruce,
doves fluttering.

I am grandmother walking past school,
waving to children, businessperson
passing new car lot wondering
how much profit will accrue,
teenager appreciating color and lines
of red sports car.

I unlock office door,
put lilac in water, turn on lights,
pick up pen and become poet
before turning on calculator.

All these I am before morning coffee.
Who knows whom I might be by night?

WANDERING THOUGHTS

Peel stickers
from shiny paper,
affix them to mailers
to be stuffed
into envelopes;

choreograph movements,
peel, align, rub,
toss into pile,
reach for stickers,

13

peel, align, rub...

Soon hands, alone,
will perform,
and mind meander
free from the tedium
of now,
see everything
in Technicolor.

There is no task
in which
there is no poem.

SOLUTION TO LIFE'S PROBLEMS

Address labels
meant to stick to envelopes
want to curl
around fingers,
adhere to one
like persons and events
preferably avoided.

Arrange
labeled and stuffed
mailers
in boxes, neatly,
so they will march
like soldiers
through
postage meter.

If lives
might be squared up
and systematized
would we be
settled and happy?

IF THERE WERE JUST A FORMULA

She enters pluses and minuses,
presses button
with asterisk.
Two zeros appear.
She turns off calculator
for she is finished.

Outside the office
she never knows
when she is finished.
Has she said enough,
cleaned enough,
baked enough,
helped enough?

Where is balance
between credits of her giving
and debits of her own needs?

TAKE RESPONSIBILITY

Friday afternoon at four
the weekend calls.
Try to block out thoughts
of fishing, golfing,
dining, reading, bridge.

Concentrate
just one more hour.

EIGHTEENTH FLOOR RECEPTIONIST

Blonde hair moussed into wedge,
smoothed over ears,
accentuates a pointed chin.

Eye shadow, lip gloss
are artfully casual.
They might have taken scissors
and snipped her, full-blown,
from a page of Vogue.

She smiles as we enter,
asks names, motions to chairs;
offers coffee,
brings it from somewhere
wearing silk shirt,
soft black pants cinched at waist
and again at ankles
above shiny pumps.

    "L and L Consultants. Good afternoon.
    He is in conference now. May I take
    a message?"
    "L and L Consultants. Good afternoon.
    Yes he is. May I ask who is calling?"

Such poise, such presence
in one so young.
She might be my daughter--
granddaughter almost.

I remember my first job.
Untutored, trying too hard to please,
certainly I babbled.

PIANIST ON MY ROOF

Various sounds drift down--
mechanized droning tone
when she vacuums,
water swooshing in pipes
after she bathes her child,
tuneless concerts
by tiny fingers,
little feet running.

I look up
from papers on the desk,
relax.
Recordings, I thought,
when first they settled in
and music became a part
of my environment.

Discordant notes
like weeds in a flower garden
prompt artist to play
a few bars over,
convince me I am audience
to "live" music."

Chopin, Mozart,
Bach, Brahms float down
as well as jazz
and contemporary things.

How lucky one is
to have a pianist on her roof.

ACCOUNTING SEMINAR

Heads spinning with technicalities
of pros and cons of various methods
of accounting for contractors,
we escape to the lounge.

Outside
a sparrow flits about,
bits and pieces in her beak
of materials for a nest;
labor, overhead,
method of accounting
of no consequence to her.

AN ACCOUNTANT SEARCHES

I am a no-nonsense calculator
    proving and balancing,
an unlocked door
    welcoming ideas,
a light
    waiting to be turned on,
a faucet
    spewing hot and cold,
a pen
    writing sometimes smoothly,
    sometimes blotting.

I am a letter opener
    plunging into information
    both informative and insipid,
a mailbox
    gathering whatever comes.

I am sorting it out.

MY CUP RUNNETH OVER

Grandchildren
gave me a mug;
its imprint:
THE SUCCESSFUL WOMAN.
Their mother bought it
of course.
Does she think
me successful?
Do they?
Does the world?
Do I?

Daughters
invite me to lunch
and on shopping trips.
Grandchildren
slip away from parents
to snuggle against me.
Brothers hug me
at family reunions.
A client said
my effort saved him
several thousand dollars.

I count no soul an enemy.
Successful enough.

TO MY LITTLE FRIENDS

I watch for you, and when you smile
as you go past in single file
and wave your mittened hands to me
it makes me happy as can be.

TWELVE KIDS ON A ROPE

They are coming--
chattering, laughing;
little persons clutching
colorful blocks strung
on a rope.

Teachers hold each end,
direct them to
"big" school for lunch.
At "Little Peoples"
they learn to care and share.

For years our grandchildren
on that rope looked up
to my office window and smiled.
By spring their peers
were waving to "Grandma."

Today, first day of school,
only teacher smiles.
Kindergarten has claimed
my youngest descendant.

THE ARTS--HERS AND MINE

I was astounded
my rosemaling friend
had not a dictionary
until it occurred to me--
I have no paintbrush.

SHELVES OF POETS

Anthologies have one place,
complete works or chapbooks
of individual poets another.

English friend, Barbara Stevens,
would have smiled to know
she stands separated from Shakespeare
by Shel Silverstein.

Instructor Michael Dennis Browne
is shelved beside Elizabeth Browning's
"Sonnets from the Portuguese."

Dear Meg Kramer
whose arthritic fingers
curl around her pen
inspires me,
is flanked by Keats
and Edgar Lee Masters.

Lila Borg Rohrer,
writer of lusty love poems,
leans on Dr. Seuss.

Roy Benjamin Moore,
whose work made us laugh--
or cry--
would have appreciated
proximity to Ogden Nash.

All these, and more,
fill the ledges of my library
and the layers
of my soul.

IF I WERE TO DO WATER COLOR

I would have the courage
to paint the near side yellow,
the off side orange,
to give dimension to houses.

I would paint reflections
in rivers
holding darkly blue images,
upside-down;

water that shows shades of blue,
turquoise and purple--
white where brown-bodied children
stomp and splash;

roses that are
faintly pink at edges,
crimson at their vortex centers
like those of Georgia O-Keeffe.

I would define straight lines.
I tried one time,
and colors chose to run
like coffee stain spreading.

I would paint likenesses
that stir
memory and soul!

I have not time
to perfect
the stroke of brush.

I will try
to do it with words.

IN MY SHARING

"Only the poet can, with simple pencil and paper,
offer the ocean in words so full of water that readers
drip and taste salt."
From "Ocean Artistry" by Debbie Parvin

I tell you the mountain
    feel loftiness
    shudder at steep cliffs
    breathe thin air
    listen for waterfalls
    see forever

I tell you the oak tree
    imagine photosynthesis
    watch squirrel climb rough bark
    perceive round-edged leaves
    envision bird nests
    inhale shade

I tell you the lake
    ignore motor noise--
        hear silence of sails
    intuit motion of swimming things
    imagine water lilies
    ignite your being at the firefly
    ride the warble of the loon

I tell you the child
    smell unkempt hair
    embrace sturdy torso
    touch the spirit of his running
    rise with the flight of her dance
    know pure exuberance
    swallow gourmet innocence

I tell you these things
that we may taste them together

TAKE YOUR PEN IN HAND

Not only must enlightened persons
publish their theses.
You and I must write
so that all we have known and been
does not fall with us to our graves.

Do it!
Scribble down the recipe your children love
even if you write, "A pinch of this
and a dribble of that."
How will they taste it when you are gone
if you do not?

Identify those photos--
names, dates.
Write a background for Uncle Joe,
third from left, back row.
Earmark Grandma so everyone knows
who flashed that benevolent smile.

Do not pen just knobby kneed facts.
Write feelings and emotions
you may not even know you know
when you begin.

We need not delve
into the meaning of life.
We will never be Emily Dickinsons.
No matter.
Our descendants will know us better
and be richer.

And, just maybe,
we will learn about ourselves.

WHAT IS A sme?

It is I.

In typing correspondence,
employer's initials, upper case,
preceded mine, lower case.

So they called me Sme--
rhymed with she.

I never longed to be
upper case SME,
that designation reserved
for employers and dignitaries
like LBJ and JFK.

To publish collections of poems
smeBOOKS was born
and I am ceo!

VARIOUS ABODES

Long since abandoned, birth home sheltered
large farm family sixteen years.

I cooked, cleaned, washed and ironed
as barter for room and board
in high-ceilinged brick house
that I might attend high school in town;
lived with widow while hired girl
and baby sitter for pastor's wife.

As fledgling secretary
I shared bedroom and kitchen privileges
with girlfriend.
Confident in housekeeping ability
we moved to basement apartment.

100 year old home as a bride had no plumbing,
has been razed along with barns and grove.
First daughter was born there.

A new house replaces our first apartment.
Across town, first upstairs, then down,
we resided in a four-plex.

I made lefse on the stovetop
of wood range in next home in the country.
Landlady upstairs took colicky second baby
to her quarters sometimes.

We built a new house;
sawed, painted, varnished, laid tile
while living in two rooms--
then sold it.

Three daughters shouted through register
to little boys downstairs
when we bought the duplex.

Family room and bath were added
soon after buying present home.
Birthdays, holidays, graduations
have been celebrated.

Daughters married ,
made homes of their own.

With just Dad and I left,
we built an unnecessary room
where we spend most of our time.

MY OWN ROOM

Seventh in family of nine,
I roomed with sisters,
hired girl to elderly couple,
with the eighty-year old aunt;
intent on education, with stranger
who became friend.

Married young, I welcomed sharing with spouse.
While working woman, wife, mother,
extra rooms filled first with daughters,
later sewing machine and guest accommodations.

Today bed and dresser are gone--
replaced by sofa bed, file cabinets,
bookcases, word processor, copy machine.
I revel in my space.
Now I must really write that book.

PICTURE OF CONTROVERSY

You stand forever by the wall of stone.
A nurse, a teacher, shop owner--adults
demand I take the picture down, disown
the curse of my photography; results
I think, fine likeness of your teens
when you all lived with me before you wed;
when trinkets, sweaters, slips, crew sox, blue jeans
all grew into great piles on chair and bed.

It hangs above my word processor now
and will as long as I have any say.
Harangue me, if you must and then allow
you're still my little girls, even today.

Some times when I sit down to read or write
my rhymes, I see you all tucked in at night.

27

CHECK-OUT PERSONNEL AT SUPER MARKET

Arrive before shift
in red shirt, black pants uniform,
verify that drawer contains specified amount,
turn to greet first customer,
smile...

turn each item so bar code activates register,
smooth out lumpy packages of potatoes
until beep announces it has been read,
place produce on scale,
punch keys for designation and price,
call for customer service person to sack--
or reach for plastic bag--
canned goods on bottom, bread on top...

explain newly-installed
credit card/food stamp machine,
determine who merits senior discount Wednesdays,
announce total...
wait while customer writes check,
often adding to amount
for cash in hand...or lotto tickets.
Stand patiently as some
count money from purse to the penny.

Place sacked groceries
in numbered basket,
give matching number to customer,
push basket through door
to outside pickup.

At slow times, spray cleaner
on conveyer belt, wipe it off,
stock end caps near by
or push abandoned carts
to their places...

turn to next customer
smile
ring up
sack
make change and/or small talk,
remind them to take numbers.

Next.

APPRECIATING NURSES

white clad
efficient, kind
watching monitors
rubbing backs
filling forms
taking temps
and sometimes abuse

surrounded by
blinking lights
beeping buzzers
confused patients
concerned kin

apologizing
for pricks in the arm
cold stethoscopes
and for waking one

recording input and output
effectualizing doctors' orders
and what patients request

caring for those who will live
comforting those who will die
trying to remain objective
paying in emotion
only they know

SMALL BUSINESS ENTREPRENEURS

Often women,
they deliver kids to school or day care
before arriving at store.

Owner and employees
share tasks--make coffee,
turn on lights, put cash in drawer,
dust, vacuum, straighten merchandise.

Potential customers are greeted,
assisted in finding wants or needs,
offered suggestions.

Uniqueness and service are paramount...
gift wrapping, bridal registries,
take-home-on-approval.

Trips to market--both fun and work--
allow view of what is new,
demand decisions as to what
small-town customers will buy.

Delivery persons deposit boxes
to be opened and unpacked,
checked for defects, priced
(after finding elusive packing slips.)
Merchandise is assigned places
and plastic peanuts litter the floor.

Unforeseen frustration is being told,
"Please stay on hold for the next
available service rep,"
when phoning to request credit
for breakage or damage.

One satisfied customer
erases that memory.

WOMEN OF TUESDAY AND THURSDAY

We meet twice a week for our coffee and toast--
about fourteen members of whom we can boast.
We're seldom that many on any one day;
if someone would join us, she knows that she may.
We're mostly retailers, but one is a baker,
and one an accountant and one survey-taker.
One manages Chamber, one Savings and Loan.
One publishes news. In three years we've grown.
We welcome new faces. A recent addition
is teaching gymnastics to kids as her mission.
We gather together, supporting each other
discussing our children, our work and our brother;
examine the boards of the school, county, city,
decide if Bill Cosby or Carson's more witty.

No topic's too weighty, nor any too light.
We talk of what's wrong in the world and what's right;
of things that we did back when we were young,
of lullabies, ditties and songs we have sung,
of things that should never have happened to us,
of why this or that cause our husbands to fuss,
of birthings and deaths, of burials, cremations,
of business, fashions, dressmakers' creations,
of puppies and kittens and antics of pets,
of children determined to watch TV sets,
of things we enjoy and things that are frightening
like cancer and AIDS, tornadoes and lightning.
Sometimes we are serious and sometimes we're silly.
We've wondered whose pickles are really most dilly.

These bi-weekly meetings are not frivolous.
They make daily living less stressful for us.

31

APPLES, APPALOOSAS AND FORGET-ME-NOTS

Like Alice, I descend to alien world,
leave behind a place where words are art.
enter shop where strange sights are.
Glass vials hold powders named apple,
cranberry, shell, pecan, buttercup, cornflower.
Painters mix oil with those exotic colors
to consistency of toothpaste.

Plates, vases, figurines, pitchers,
cups and saucers line shelves.
I hear foreign-sounding words:
blanks, scrolls, terp, kiln, cones, liners, shaders.
Curiouser and curiouser!

Deft hands choose sable brushes
  that lie in rows in boxes,
dip them into blobs of color
arranged on gridded glass palettes.

Instructor turns perfume bottle in her hand,
studies it, brush held aloft, plans its decoration.
She rolls it on the table, adds color to the narrow neck,
braces finger, wipes out forget-me-nots,
dabs removed color on napkin.
From wide brush, rose blush flows down
rounded sides of bottle.

Accomplished artist dabs freckles
on wild-maned appaloosa on vase already fired.
Indian Chief with flowing hair adorns the other side.

Second week advisor paints rose/american beauty
over fired bottle, highlights leaves with moss/black green.
Little finger anchored,
she touches minuscule dots at centers of flowers.

Beginner paints wild roses--
required first project before forget-me-nots.
Teacher advises use of wide brush to draw

petal color to yellow center, lightly,
like touch of butterfly wings;
shows her how to pull highlights with wipeout tool,
touch tiny black dots between petals.

Red of another's apples flows down
to green, certainly crisp, undersides.
After firing, he will cover with redder red
the apples and the cardinal. With chin in hand
he holds plate beside illustration,
passes it to mentor. "The Master,"
he calls her when she smoothes a few strokes.
"I just want to remain Teacher," she grins.

Flexible palette knives scrape drying color into a pile.
A drop of oil renews it.
Hands continue to stroke detail as conversation flows:
moving-day experiences, kids' schnauzer-poodle,
teenager's drivers' permit.

Vase painter strokes background of stars on flag
to be foil for magnificent horse,
adds darker tone to Indian Chief's features--
says he looks too Norwegian--
deems the project ready for firing, covers her palette,
places a plastic hood over the work.

I walk home, the sky a porcelain bowl upside-down.
Light blues and grays wash into each other
like background of the plate.
White fluffs have been wiped out overhead
like huge, puffy forget-me-nots,
grayness west is edged with silver/white,
resembles mane of the appaloosa.
As if the bowl had been fired
then brushed with wide, white strokes,
sunbeams fan out from setting sun
to streak, but not obliterate, the clouds.

Perhaps I must observe a ballet class to enhance
appreciation of flight of birds.

RESPONSE TO A PERSON APOLOGIZING

You have apologized enough;
borne guilt for things you need not,
done nothing consciously to hurt,
sidestepped possibilities
to accept responsibility.

You are not in charge of the universe
nor is it tied to your apron,
so you need not apologize
for famine in Africa.
Of course you care!
Though you grieve for them,
you have seen
that your own were fed.

What if from your home
spring leaders or molders of minds?
If you have sent them out whole
have you not contributed?

FOOTLOOSE?

One year they're flat,
the next high heel;
does anyone
care how they feel?

The toes are round,
then sharp or square;
feet never know
how they will fare.

I'm not concerned
what "style" may be.
My loafers still
are fine for me.

INTRUSION OR INCLUSION?

Her regal bearing and her silver hair,
her cultured voice, possessions brought next door
bespoke, perhaps, a person who might share
no daily conversations on our floor.

At eighty-four she'd likely be aloof
and set in ways as elderly can be.
Would she view others' customs with reproof
or, even worse, endure us silently?

Apartment life begets a sense of clan,
of fellowship, almost of family.
A one-time teacher, just as I, how can
I make her welcome, so that she'll feel free

to ask for help, to let us be her friend?
Why had I worried? After I had met
her in the hall I knew a dividend
for all the rest of us had just been set.

A young man exited the door beyond
(his darker skin betrayed his foreign birth.)
I thought she might, as I, become quite fond
of one more student if she knew his worth.

I could not quickly bring to mind his name.
"My name is Fahlah," he informed with grace.
"How's that again?" she asked, and who could blame
this senior neighbor, newly in this place?

She looked into his eyes, inches above
and cupped her blue-veined hands about his head.
Delightful wit erupted we would love.
"I think that I shall call you Bob, she said.

ALL THAT FREE TIME

The days are counting down;
fourteen, to be exact,
until I close the door.
Just how will I react

to freedom of my self
from deadlines and routine;
from serving others' needs?
Will thought process stay keen?

This plateau, so they say--
this long-awaited time--
the ending of life work
(and I still in my prime)

brings days not scheduled out.
I'll go to malls and shop,
play bridge or golf, or read;
eat sundaes with fudge top.

Talk shows and TV "soaps"
hold not much lure for me.
My kitchen is a dream,
is almost effort-free.

I'll read the daily news,
decode the cryptoquote,
go see my aged aunt,
know issues when I vote.

I'll learn a foreign language,
dust off piano keys,
go touring in Alaska,
walk barefoot in the breeze,

take grandchildren to movies
or fishing at the lake,

sew curtains for the guest room,
make jelly, can and bake.

I'll not go crazy cleaning--
how dusty can it be?
I could arrange the closets
for more efficiency.

I may decide to garden
or really write that book.
I think I can retire
without a backward look.

APRIL EMPLOYMENT

It is now a storeroom,
the office I once occupied;
retains the blue curtain
I hung, and left when I retired.

Temporary receptionist
in front room today,
I take messages, greet persons
who were my clients.

They have redecorated here,
but the awful aqua tile
remains in the rest room.
Apartments I watched built
across the street
are dwarfed by trees planted then;
flag still flies at VFW.

As some things change
so are some constant.
Businesses come and go
but proprietors still annually visit
accountants preparing income tax.

DECISIONS, DECISIONS

Hands poised above the dummy's cards arrayed
in rows, would spade
finesse or heart
prove to be smart--

or even, lead the club, hope for a split?
She ponders it.
With steady hand
just takes command.

She cannot hear her partner's silent plea.
We all agree
it's just for fun.
She goes down one.

LEARNED FROM MEDDLING

"If you want truly to understand something,
try to change it."   Kurt Lewin

I did not like the way it was;
I thought I had to change it.
I altered here, adjusted there
and then I rearranged it.

This did not work; that was bizarre.
Another way, repulsive.
I might have ripped it all to bits
if I were more compulsive.

The longer that I worked with it
the more I knew frustration.
I came, at last, to realize
it was a good creation.

TO US
(For Toastmasters)

As one by one we stand
palms wet, and legs atremble,
we utter things not planned
when we assemble.

We all hear one same drum;
it is a proven process.
We learn to not say, "um..."
well, not to excess.

Evaluating peers,
we grow along with speaker.
No one has left in tears
nor become weaker.

Support is what we do--
self-confidence is growing.
We now can speak on cue
with syntax flowing.

MORNING ABLUTION

Go alone to the hilltop.
Face skyward
inhale clouds
bathe in fluff of wildflowers
reach up to breeze on skin
watch sunlight play on tree trunks
lean toward nature sounds
sense the scent of things growing
taste solitude and serenity.

Have no purpose but to be
and be visited
by your inner self.

WHEN LIFE GIVES YOU LEMONS

Perfectly fluted, light brown crust,
iridescent filling, fluffy, moist meringue;
this pie, not from a box,
tenderly rolled, stirred and baked
delights eye and palate.

A lemon--yellow, fragrant,
softer than those from the store--
is on my counter, tree-ripened,
hand-picked by friend on vacation,
brought back to snow country, shared.

Tomorrow it will become that pie--
or a reasonable facsimile.

KITCHEN HELP

French dressing whipped,
she emits an anguished cry.
For years she mashed veggies
for babies, now mothers.

She ground graham crackers for crusts,
soda crackers for coating fish;
pureed pears for seafoam salad,
made eggnog for groggy kids;
whipped batters at low speed,
filling for cream pie on high.

Perhaps a transplant would allow
extended life (a new motor
beneath her chrome skirt.)

Modern ones are plastic with ten speeds--
She did all we needed
with two.

THE FLU

I'm slightly nauseous,
don't want to get busy
and when I stand or walk
I'm rather dizzy.

There are these aches
in stomach, shoulders, back;
of just such symptoms
knowledge is quite slack.

I can't remember...
shall I starve or feed it?
I only know
I certainly don't need it.

A SMILE IN THE NIGHT

Up and doing--coming, going--
body responds, works efficiently;
mind over matter.

Prone, at night, pressures close in--
relationships, menus, meetings,
world news, housekeeping,
record keeping.
Aches and pains make lumps in pillow,
tangle sheets at my feet,
and the clock makes that droning sound.

A conscious smile--forced, wide,
until I feel it in my eyes--
somehow lifts chin,
straightens spine, relaxes muscles,
deepens breathing,
and knots under my rib cage
untangle.

RESPONDING TO ADS IN WOMEN'S MAGAZINES

Hands get the extra help they need
   --are the kids making their beds?
Nothing's more fitting
   --than a size 12 when a ten goes on a binge
The balm for life's litttle ups and downs
   --do you have something for the big ones?
In your hands it can change the tempo
   --I'd just like to change the channel
Like the touch of a caressing breeze
   --the wind blew down the birdhouse
Maybe she's born with it
   --and maybe it came from a bottle
The blondest blonde you can be
   --my grandchildren wouldn't know me
When you're comfortable you can really go places
   --car pool, dentist, grocery store, little league
Designed to fit a woman
   --a woman like me or like Dolly?
The body comes to its senses
   --in THAT?
Hands that have nothing to hide
   --not even Easter eggs?
For just the problems you have
   --can it fix drippy faucets?
so simple, so personal
   --so EXPENSIVE1
Now doesn't that feel better?
   --not as good as flannel pajamas
Good for life
   --just get me through today
Don't take our word for it
   --I didn't plan to

WE CAN'T KEEP UP IN MINNESOTA

We spent, I know, a million dollars
on blouses with long, pointy collars.

Then ruffled necks were all the go--
we've quite a few of those to throw.

One year "big shirts" were very "in;"
they did not make a soul look thin.

And have you seen (it makes me cry)
the skirts are now about mid-thigh.

When in Midwest a style we boast,
it's very "out" on either coast.

YOU KNOW I'M OVER FIFTY

Though hats have now
come back in style
they're not worn by
the rank and file.

The models, yes,
and teenage girls
will perch them on
their jaunty curls;

but I'll not rush
right out to get
a hat to spoil
my shampoo-set.

REMODELING DREAM

Formica chips rattle, floor samples dance,
ivy paper covers the edge of my restless night.
Tunnel in ceiling where ductwork will be
enters cave mouth where wall is knocked out.
Glassware and cups jump from boxes
for transport to new home.
Faucets drip tears into sink, know
they are delegated to the garage.

Tupperware containers are jaunty,
will inhabit new cupboards.
Small appliances on counter smile,
their residence on pull-out shelves assured.
Accent pieces parade with potholders, dishtowels,
look for their places.
Sugar, flour, spices lobby to be near
baking center, say that will save steps.

Wood-burning heater belches smoke,
resists replacement by gas-log fireplace.
Carpet samples dart from room to room,
juxtapose with chairs and other-colored floors.
Nuances of colors I have chosen--
even white in varying degrees--
close around me like a shroud.

Daughters with eye for style and design
offer suggestions, then affirm ,
"It's your kitchen."
Interior Decorator knocks at door
of consciousness, but I reject her.
I shall live with mistakes and/or touches of genius
of my own choosing.

GENERATION GAP CLOSES

Doilies on settee arms
conjure image
of sheets flapping on lines.

Aunt is shaking hand-braided rugs,
moving fern stand and knitting basket,
scurrying with broom and dustpan.
She picks up velvet-covered photo albums,
polishes rolltop desk, centers revolving stool
before player piano.

Bedrooms smell of fresh sheets
beneath hand-quilted spreads.
Embroidered towels
hang behind pitcher and bowl
in dry sink.
Ancestors' pictures
in ornate frames grace walls
and top of chiffonier.

Grandma sets teakettle on wood stove,
places fresh cinnamon rolls in warming oven,
takes down teapot, shakes in leaves,
pours boiling water over to steep
under a cozy.

We will drink from cups that were bonuses
in oatmeal boxes,
spread home-churned butter on hot rolls.

Married, I decorated my home
contemporary style.

Daughters search antique stores
for pitchers and bowls, lace doilies,
fern stands and depression glass
that came, free, in oatmeal boxes.

GRANDMOTHER PROFILES

Grandmother wore print cotton dresses, sensible shoes.
Her hair was a bun at the nape of her neck
held in place with hairpins.
She rolled my hair in rags to make it curl.
Her kitchen smelled of fresh-baked bread
and there was flour on her apron.
She lined jars of home-canned fruits and vegetables
in a palette of colors on cellar shelves,
sewed quilts for all the beds, crocheted doilies,
squinted her eyes to thread a needle,
raised chickens, prepared huge Sunday dinners,
and even bigger ones for Thanksgiving and Christmas;
her pie crust melted in your mouth.
She set milk at back of the stove to become cottage cheese.
It took all day.
She sewed little coats for grandchildren
using wool from coats the aunts discarded,
scrubbed floors with floppy rag mops.
She gave lots of hugs.

My daughters' children's Grandma wears heels to work,
sweat suits at home in the evening.
She brushes her hair, holds it in place with spray.
Sometimes her kitchen smells like fresh-baked bread
but she uses frozen loaves and doesn't wear an apron.
Her canning is a row of jellies that sparkle like a rainbow.
She sews little quilts for grandbabies,
writes poems and reads a lot,
wears glasses with three sections,
goes to an office every day and has candy
for when kids stop in.
She likes to go out for Sunday dinner
but makes turkey and dressing for Thanksgiving.
She bakes bread pudding in the microwave.
It takes twenty minutes.
She plays golf sometimes; bridge too.
She gives lots of hugs.

REQUEST

When you think of me
in your garden of friends
don't place me in a row
with a stick at the end
that says:
"zinnia."

Rather, imagine me scattered
throughout your garden;
for on some days
I might be a daisy
and on others, a rose.

A THUMBNAIL SKETCH OF ME

I am generous, and perfection
is my everlasting goal.
I have a deep appreciation of
the arts and music,
an ability to sense and know
higher truth.

I will always be successful
in my professional career,
be involved in many gatherings,
parties and communications.
I will soon be honored
by someone I respect,
and my name will be famous
in the future.

It must be true.
Fortune cookies have said it was so.
I save only those that flatter me.

A NEW BEGINNING

How bittersweet the memories she holds
close to herself as she assigns a place
for forty years' accumulation; folds
a towel that had pillowed fragile vase.

She'd stripped the paint from Grandma's old sideboard
that Grandpa'd built from wooden crates those years
ago. A treasure now with one accord
her helpers all agree. It barely clears

the door through which her sons with loving care
are transporting her heirlooms and her everyday
necessities, the dishes and the bear
she keeps for grandkids who will come to play.

She hears them now upstairs in her west room
that may one day be where she sews, or stores
the quilts she makes for gifts. She can't assume
that this year she'll have time from classroom chores

to finish handmade crafts. She's proud inside
that after half a century she'd willed
herself to seek employment, then decide
that teaching might be where she'd be most skilled.

With more than just a small amount of pluck
she'd left her home, and joined the college force
to graduate with honors 'till today a truck
full of her past is emptying. Remorse

is absent as her family surround
her physically. Emotional support
is obvious and family jokes abound.
Grown kids give hugs and little ones cavort.

She'd never thought mid-life she'd be alone
collecting from the various domiciles

her treasures that had been on family loan,
and truck them off across those many miles

to where she is employed, and grateful for
this house, available for one year lease.
She'll stay her year and maybe even more;
her first week pangs at school will surely cease.

She takes her crew downtown to dine at noon.
A group that size in small towns makes a stir.
She tells the locals who she is and soon
their greeting hands reach out to welcome her.

SONG TO MY SOUL

How well this shell has served me--
not as cocoon, obliterating,
but rather as blanket
holding me together.

Bones, sinew, muscles, veins
special female place where little tadpoles
that sprouted tiny arms and legs became babies,
cavern that adjusted to removal
of organs and insertion of a clock,
skin, self-healing
comprise what you see.

But that is not "I."
"I" am who holds the pen,
ponders, grieves, exalts,
does good things and bad;
makes decisions, is hard headed,
looks forward;
who sometimes regrets, more often rejoices,
lives, wide-eyed,
knows that one day she will shed the shell
and that she will be content.

ETHEREAL REUNIONS

A gathering of persons, atmosphere
of expectancy,
heavy air, green benches;
those at desks behind gridded windows
oblivious to coughs, muted greetings, crumbs
on floor from lunches carried.

We wait long.
They come through the door, eyes searching.
Child runs forward, reaches up
to haggard-looking young man.
Girl with long hair steps from the ranks,
waits to be spotted,
becomes entangled with arms, legs, lips.
Matron wipes tears, embraces son.

Woman in print cotton dress,
hair wound tightly to head
moves to incoming tide to brush
against arm of man who,
at her touch glances down.
Fingers twined, they melt into the throng.

I wake before I know
for whom I wait.

TIME OUT

I savor scent of coffee,
sip leisurely.

With floor wiped up,
clean clothes folded,
push aside
niggling thoughts
of other chores to do--

bathroom to clean,
furniture to polish,
groceries to buy--
for I have a whole day.

Accustomed to readying
for entertaining
in a half-day or evening
during employment years,
I have a fuzzy feeling--
a sort of contentment--
that I am master of my hours and minutes.

Golden years
have arrived--
and I was ready.

GUARDIANS OF MY LIFE

My childhood yard
was full of them--
angels in three sizes,
small, medium, tiny,
outlined
in moonlight silver.

I could see them
from my window,
remember our exuberance
creating them,
taste snow on my tongue,
feel it down my neck.

Tonight there is one angel--
much larger.
I am grateful for the hand
that helped me
to my feet.

51

VANQUISHING A MISINTERPRETATION
(AFTER FORTY YEARS)

Tune on local radio
is dedicated to my granddaughter
by a peer.

Stigma of being "farm kid"
I remember from youth
is gone.

Any stupid act or statement
was put down by retort,
"dumb farmer."

Epithet was never actually leveled
at me, steady student, trying
too hard.

At class reunions I am embraced.
Was the slur merely something to say,
impersonal?

How many persons have been
demoralized by flip generalizations
and labels?

PUTTING AN OLD HURT TO REST

As I count knives, spoons and forks
to be certain none is in the garbage
before filing them in the box
for future "company" use,
I forgive the maiden aunts
for counting silverware in my childhood
when I thought that they thought
we might have slipped them
into our pockets.

NO SOUR CREAM TODAY

Forty years ago
I thought I'd know
I was rich if ever I could buy
sour cream on impulse.

Today I may.
I might even purchase
beefsteak.

My doctor checked
my cholesterol.
My cart contains
skinned chicken breasts
and margarine.

5% OFF FOR SENIORS

Prematurely gray,
I refused to grocery shop
on Wednesday,
the day those teen-aged girls
at the checkout asked,
"Do you get the discount?"

Today, at sixty-two
I do.

WEIGHTY RATIONALIZATION

Just cornflakes with raisins,
no sugar,
skim milk;

a luncheon-time trade-off
to warrant
pecan pie.

TO PAPERBACK AUTHORS

I am not old.
At sixty-six I relax
in novels of various genres.
You designate women my age
"old ladies."
Old is a state
perceived by young people.

I do not need lily-white heroines,
appreciate flaws in character
you correctly interject.
But sex is a personal enjoyment,
not a spectator sport.

Four-letter words
do not shock or anger me.
They make me tired.

OLYMPIC COMPETITION

Supple, slender, scantily clad
they glide, turn, twist, swirl,
leap, almost fly.
Showing presence, poise,
they reach, skip, land smoothly,
smile.

I never could glide,
could barely stand
on those thin blades.
They swoop across the screen,
bend down, retrieve flowers.

There is no gold medal
for cross stitch.

SLIGHT COMPENSATION

I reach down,
unplug sweeper.
Sudden pain riddles my back,
head feels light,
stomach queasy.

Slow step by slow step,
I ease into a chair,
gasp great gulps of air.
Room whirls.
Unable to lay handle down,
I hold it,
cord a snake before me.

I move forward, lessen pressure,
stand, twist, find I can walk.
It certainly takes my mind off
arthritis in my arms.

CAN THIS BE?

I've had pride,
more energy than some;
been involved, try to be
all things to all persons;
keep healthy,
exercise, eat sensibly;
play a B+ hand of bridge,
a C- round of golf.

My hair is gray;
stray strands appeared at twenty.
Brown spots spatter hands and wrists.
This morning I glanced in a mirror.
My mother gazed back at me.

OLD AGE IS NOT THE PITS

A little bit of arthritis
has crept into my hands.
My eyes depend on tri-focals;
the hourglass drips its sands.

I wake each night with hot flashes.
I have a tricky hip .
I take blood pressure pills daily.
A coldsore blights my lip.

My pacemaker keeps me steady,
alleviating fears.
Retirement checks arrive monthly--
We've earned them through the years.

Our grandchildren are a blessing,
our daughters keep us young.
Our sons-in-law are true treasures,
perhaps 'till now unsung.

While years ago my concern was,
"I cannot die just yet;
my little girls need their mother."
That duty has been met.

The longer I live, more fully
I savor every day.
From this side of three-and-sixty,
Old age calls. It's O.K.

AUTOBIOGRAPHY

An artless, affable awkward apprentice American
avidly ascending, aspiring, altruistic,
accepting acclaim after average accomplishments
amongst admiring adults;

an audacious adolescent,
absolute, academic, adhering,
aghast at atheism, abuse,
anarchies, atrocities,
atomic aggression,
avarice, arrogance, alcoholism.

An awakening adult,
ambitious, almost assertive,
actually attempting altering attitudes;
assessing archaic authority, austerity,
assumptions and ambiguities;
arguing away animosities,
abandoning annoyance at atypical activity,
according acceptance (albeit against approval)
about another's antics, another's anthem;

Achieving autonomy.

Aging, advancing,
aroused, attuned,
admitting ambivalence;
acknowledging age-old accusations :
Are affirmation, assent advisable?
Are abrasive actions always acceptable?
Are abberant advocates allowed alarming accord?
Aren't admonitions advisable against adverse addicts?
Are abnormal, atypical artists accountable?

Agonizing, analyzing,
aching after assurance,
appreciating, applauding,
admiring, adoring,
apologizing, articulating, asking...
I am.

CHRISTMAS LISTS

For fifty years
I've kept them--
columns
with dates at top;
check mark when I send
circled when we receive.

At first parents, siblings,
aunts, uncles, peers;
later years, names change
in instances of marriage--
or divorce.
Children, co-workers, neighbors
swell the list;
job changes, residence moves
add others.
The adding is a blessing.

Often, of late, deletions;
Father, then Mother,
a brother, two sisters,
aunts, uncles, cousins.

Now nephews, nieces, grandchildren
in homes widespread
receive our missives,
place our names on their lists
until, inevitably one Christmas,
we shall be removed
from their registers.

Our daughters
will find my lists
and wonder, "Who was
this person, or that?"

DON'T LET MY WISDOM GO TO WASTE

As a child
I thought
the wind was brought
by tree branches trembling.

As a youth
I believed
that truth was received
by classes assembling.

As a mom
I was sure
that I could endure
being mother, employee and wife.

As a grandma
I knew
as the little ones grew
that they were the joy of my life.

As a senior
I trust
that age will be just
and allow me to share what I've learned.

Wind is free,
not controlled.
Truth and wisdom are gold.
In what's seen, heard and felt they are earned.

Supermoms
take a rest;
all those loved ones you've blessed
would be glad to share some of your duties.

And as grandmas
enjoy

every girl, every boy
and your own life besides knitting booties.

JOURNEY TO SELF

Gradually
I became myself
as opposed to
daughter, sister, wife,
mother, grandma, friend,
though those I remain,

reluctantly
conceding mortality
which cannot negate
that I have been
daughter, sister, wife,
mother, grandma, friend--
to be remembered, perhaps,
lovingly.